DATE DUE		
JUN 15 2007	MAY 2007	
JUN 27 2007		
APR 1 0 2011		

The Urbana Free Library

To renew materials call
217-367-4057

SLOW DOWN, SARA!

by Laura Driscoll

illustrated by
Page Eastburn O'Rourke

The Kane Press
New York

2-07
14.00

Acknowledgement: Our thanks to Marc Feldman, PhD (Physics, UC Berkeley), Professor, University of Rochester, for helping us make this book as accurate as possible.

Book Design/Art Direction: Edward Miller

Library of Congress Cataloging-in-Publication Data

Driscoll, Laura.
   Slow down, Sara! / by Laura Driscoll ; illustrated by Page
Eastburn O'Rourke.
      p. cm. — (Science solves it!)
   Summary: Ben is worried when his friend "Speedy" Sara slows down just before
the soapbox race, but she is using science to improve her chances.
      ISBN 1-57565-125-4 (alk. paper)
      [1. Speed—Fiction. 2. Racing—Fiction.]   I. O'Rourke, Page
Eastburn, ill. II. Title. III. Series.
   PZ7.D79Sl 2003
   [E]—dc21

                                          2002010663

10 9 8 7 6 5 4 3 2 1

First published in the United States of America in 2003 by The Kane Press.
Printed in Hong Kong.

Science Solves It! is a trademark of The Kane Press.

I pedaled my bike faster, trying to catch up with Sara.

We were headed for the park, and as usual, Sara was in a rush.

"Hey!" I called out. "Wait up!"

Sara and I have been friends forever. So I was used to her rushing everywhere. The thing was, Sara did everything fast.

She walked fast. She ran fast. She roller-bladed fast. She biked fast.

In any flat-out race, Sara could not be beat.

So, what's the *problem* with that, you may ask? I'll tell you.

At lunch, Sara was always the first one finished. But you could tell what she had eaten by looking at her shirt.

At soccer practice, she was always the first one ready. But she never looked it.

In art class, she was always the first one done. But lots of times, she got the assignment wrong.

I had tried to tell Sara to slow down about a million times. But she never seemed to hear me.

At last, I caught up to Sara in the park. "Where's the fire?" I asked her.

"Oops. Sorry, Ben," she said. "Did I leave you in the dust again?"

"Yeah, but it's okay," I said. "Dust looks good on me."

Sara didn't laugh at my joke. She wasn't listening. She was reading a poster on the park notice board.

"Hey, Sara. A *race*," I said. "You should enter. You race everywhere, anyway."

SOAPBOX DERBY!

WHO: Kids, ages 7 to 9

WHERE: Park Hill

WHEN: Saturday, June 12, 2:00 P.M.

HOW: Build your own gravity-powered car. That means no motors allowed!

COME READY TO RACE!

EART
DAY
EVER
Recy
Re

Park Hill Festiva
Family Pi
Performa
Balloor
specia

I tried to nudge Sara with my elbow. But there was no Sara to nudge. I looked around. She was gone.

I had a feeling I knew where Sara was going—and what she was up to.

The next afternoon, Sara showed me the soapbox racer she had built—in one day!

I was impressed, but worried. Sara's car looked kind of . . . crooked.

"Will that make it down the hill?" I asked. I was only *half* joking.

"Ha, ha," Sara replied. "Very funny."

Sara rolled the racer to the top of her driveway. "You're just in time for the first test-drive," she said.

She climbed in and I gave her car a little push. It wobbled a few feet down the driveway, veering to the right.

It rolled onto the grass.

It tipped over on its side—and all four wheels fell off.

I ran over to Sara. "Are you okay?"

For a few seconds, Sara just lay there on the grass. Then she said, "Hmm . . . If I want to win that race, I'll need to spend more time building my car. I guess I'll have to slow down."

Sara? Slow down? Now, *this* I had to see.

The next time I saw Sara, her car was in pieces and she was surfing the web.

"I want to find out how to make my car really fast," Sara said. She was scrolling so quickly, I only made out one word—friction.

"What's friction?" I asked.

"Come on!" she said, pulling me to the door. "I want to try something."

Sara got out her brother's dirt bike. I hopped on my bike and followed her to Park Hill. "Let's race," Sara said. "But no pedaling. Deal?"

I shrugged. Whatever. Sara was sure to win, anyway.

Whenever two things rub together, friction is made. It's a force that slows things down.

"Ready, set, go!" Sara said. We coasted down the hill. Slowly but surely, my bike inched ahead! I reached the bottom way before Sara.

The rougher two things are, the more friction there is when they rub together. So when a dirt-bike tread rubs against the ground, it makes more friction than a smooth tread does. More friction, less speed!

"Whoo-hoo!" I yelled. "I win! I win!"

I had *never* beaten Sara in a race before.

But all Sara said was, "Great. Thanks, Ben." Then she rode off toward her house.

Just then, my brother Jake rode by. "Jake!" I yelled. "I beat Sara down Park Hill!"

Jake raised his eyebrows. "You? Beat Sara? I don't think so." He rode away, laughing.

The next day, I went to the town pool with my dad. Sara was there. When she saw me, she waved. "Let's try something," she said.

"You swim on your
back like this," Sara said.
She held her arms over
her head.

"I'll swim like this,"
she said. She held her
arms out to the side.
"Let's see who gets to
the other side first."

One, two, three! We both pushed off the side
and kicked hard. I sliced through the water,
pulling ahead of Sara. I got to the other
side first!

When something moves through water or
air, it makes a kind of friction called drag.
The slimmer and smoother the object, the
less drag it creates...and the faster it goes!

"Ya-hoo!" I shouted. Sara *always* beat me in swim races. But not this time.

Again, Sara just said, "Thanks, Ben!" Then she got out of the pool, grabbed her stuff, and headed home.

Just then, my dad swam up to me.

"Dad!" I said. "Did you see that?"

"See what, Ben?" Dad said, looking around.

Bummer! No one would ever believe me.
I had beaten Sara twice in two days!

Wait a minute. *Twice* in *two days*? How
could that be? What was going on?

Then it hit me. Sara had decided to *slow
down*. And boy, had she ever! She had totally
lost her edge. And the soapbox derby was the
next day! Did slower Sara stand a chance?

On the big day, I crossed my fingers for Sara. Her car looked great. But I knew the truth. She wasn't Superfast Sara anymore.

"On your mark, get set, go!" The race was on!

Right away, three cars moved way out into the lead: Ernie Foster's, Amy Pirro's, and Sara's. Maybe I had been wrong, I thought. Speedy Sara was back! Her car was the fastest. It was pulling ahead!

Suddenly, Sara's car slowed way down. Oh, no, I thought. This was it—just as I had feared. Slower Sara couldn't hold onto the lead.

Then I saw what Sara had seen—a puddle in the middle of the road. Ernie's car rolled into the puddle, skidded, turned sideways, and came to a stop. Amy's car did the same thing.

If water gets between two surfaces, the amount of friction goes way down. When there's not enough friction between a tire and the road, there may be slipping and sliding!

But Sara didn't drive through the puddle.
She had used her brakes to slow down. She
steered *around* the puddle.

Then Sara raced on down the hill . . .
and crossed the finish line first!
Sara *had* slowed down—and she still won!

I ran over to congratulate Sara. "Thanks, Ben," she said. "And thanks for all your help."

"Help?" I said. "What help?"

"You know," Sara said. "I could tell from our bike race that smooth wheels are faster. And I found out from our swim experiment that my car should have a slim shape."

"Oh. . .uh. . .right!" I said.

Brakes work because of friction. The brake rubs against the tire, creating friction. The friction slows the wheel and then stops it from turning.

Then I understood. Sara had never lost her edge. And I hadn't really won the bike and swimming races. I should have known. There was only one reason Sara would slow down— to find out how to be *faster*!

I decided I would tease Sara about that . . .

. . .whenever I caught up to her.

I can do an experiment!

THINK LIKE A SCIENTIST

Sara thinks like a scientist—and so can you!

Scientists look for answers to questions by doing experiments. To make sure an experiment is fair, they control the variables. That means they keep everything the same except the one thing they are testing. That's what Sara tries to do.

Look Back

Sara wanted to find out if smooth wheels would make her car faster, so she planned a bike race. On page 15, how does she try to make the race a fair experiment? What variable does she control? Would the test be fair if Ben used his bike pedals?

Try This!

Do an experiment. See who can tie their shoe faster, you or a friend. Ready, set, go!

Now do the experiment again but change just one thing before you start. Here are some ideas.

- One of you holds your hands in cold water for two minutes. The other does not.

- One of you wears gloves. The other does not.

- One of you takes off your shoe. The other does not.

What did you find out? How does that one change affect who wins?